D1424924

Great Uncle Jerome

Robert

Scholastic Publications Ltd.,
10 Earlham Street, London WC2H 9RX, UK

Scholastic Inc.,
730 Broadway, New York, NY 10003, USA

Scholastic Canada Ltd.,
123 Newkirk Road, Richmond Hill,
Ontario L4C 3G5, Canada

Ashton Scholastic Pty. Ltd.,
P O Box 579, Gosford, New South Wales,
Australia

Ashton Scholastic Ltd.,
165 Marua Road, Panmure, Auckland 6,
New Zealand

First published by A & C Black (Publishers) Limited, 1990
This edition published by Scholastic Publications Ltd., 1991

Copyright © Susanna Gretz and Alison Sage 1990

ISBN 0 590 76225 7

Typeset by Spectrum Typesetting
Printed in Belgium by Proost International Book Production

# Teddybears
# eat out

## Susanna Gretz & Alison Sage

**Hippo Books**
**Scholastic Publications Limited**
London

"Are you *sure* this is where you want to eat?"
asked Great Uncle Jerome.
"Oh, yes," said William and Robert.

The snack-bar was very crowded,
but they found some seats at the back.
"I want a Cheezy Whoppa!" said William.

"What's that?" asked Great Uncle Jerome.
"It's gooey fried cheese in a bun, with tomato sauce."

"I don't like cheese," said Robert.
"But what about a Cheezy Whoppa?" said William.
"Ooh, yes," said Robert.
"But you don't like cheese," said Great Uncle Jerome.

"I only like Cheezy *Whoppas*,"
explained Robert.
Great Uncle Jerome didn't understand at all.

It took a long time to choose what they wanted.
Then the manager appeared.
"Have you finished eating?" he asked.
"Finished?" said Great Uncle. "We haven't even
started. We're waiting to be served."

"You're in the wrong place," said the manager.
"These tables are for self-service only –
and just look at the queue!"

"Oh dear," said Great Uncle,
"I'll go and get the food.  Now what was it?
A…a Whizzy Chipburger…no…"
"You can order by numbers," said William.
"It's easy; we want a 16, two 4s, a double 8
and three 7s. Oh, and a 32 and a 54 with
ice-cream. You can't go wrong."

Great Uncle Jerome waited
in the queue, muttering
numbers to himself.
"A double 16? Or was
it a double 32?"

At last it was Great Uncle's turn.
"Two 45s, one 6, one 88...
and four 32s with ice-cream," he said.
"You want *ice-cream* with four 32s?"
asked the cook.
"Yes," said Great Uncle.

The cook gave him a funny look,
and put a heap of parcels on a tray.

Meanwhile, William and Robert were getting
hungrier and hungrier.
"Look at this," said William.
"Chocolate fudge sundae...cherry pie... and wow!
Here's a competition for the Star Meal!"

"It's easy," said William. "You just scratch away the patches to see if the numbers underneath win."

Your magic number is

# 749

Just scratch the three bears shown below. If the numbers underneath match your magic number, you have won this week's

## STAR MEAL!

7  4

William started scratching...

...but just then, Great Uncle Jerome arrived.
"Our Cheezy Whoppas!" said Robert.

But what was this?
There were four ice-creams with tomato sauce.
There was a pancake with mixed vegetables,
a diet lemonade and two black coffees.

Great Uncle Jerome picked up the menu.
"Perhaps we should choose something else..."
Then he saw the Star Meal competition.
"Did you do this William?" he asked.

Great Uncle Jerome called the manager.
"It's you again, is it?" said the manager.
"I think my nephew has won one of your - ahem -
Star Meals," said Great Uncle.

The manager looked quite cross.
"You are right, sir," he said.

The manager took William up to the platform.
"I am delighted to give this week's Star Meal to...
William Bear!" he said, sounding not at all delighted.
The head waitress gave William a badge, a hat
and a kiss. Everyone clapped.

There were two Cheezy Whoppas, a thick milkshake,
a Shantyburger, two chocolate sundaes and a slice
of cherry pie. William looked a bit green.
"It's all that ice-cream and tomato sauce,"
he mumbled.

"It's a shame to waste it," said Great Uncle Jerome.
"What's a Shantyburger?"
"A giant fish finger," explained Robert.

"Not bad," said Great Uncle,
"I'll have to bring you both here again."

Great Uncle Jerome

Robert